JUST ASK!

BE DIFFERENT, BE BRAVE, BE YOU

SONIA SOTOMAYOR

ILLUSTRATED BY RAFAEL LÓPEZ

Philomel Books

To Peter Kougasian
You have taught me that a body ravaged by ALS neither
stills your brilliant wit nor changes the specialness of who
you are, nor the preciousness of what you give to others.
—S.S.

For Santiago, my mighty, little Sequoia.
—R.L.

A Letter to Readers

I was born on June 25, 1954, and in 1961, when I was seven years old, I was diagnosed with juvenile diabetes. To take care of myself, I had to do things other kids did not. Sometimes I felt different. When kids saw me giving myself a needle shot of insulin, my medicine, I knew they were curious about what I was doing. But they never asked me, my parents, or my teachers about it. I also often felt they thought I was doing something wrong.

As I grew older, I realized that there are many ways to be, that I was not alone in feeling different. I wanted to write this book to explain how differences make us stronger in a good way.

Like my experiences with diabetes, the challenges some kids face can be very hard and sometimes frustrating. Some of us have conditions that require medicines or tools to manage things that other kids never have to deal with. Some of our difficulties are not even visible to others, but they make us feel different, and we may do things that others don't understand. Yet all of these challenges often give us strength that others can't imagine.

I hope by seeing yourself or your friends in this story, you will understand that we're all different, and you will find that notion comforting and empowering. I hope too that you will recognize what we have in common. Instead of fearing our differences or ignoring them, we can shed light on them and explore them together. If you ever wonder why someone is doing something different from other kids, **Just Ask.**

Sonia Sotomayor

Hi, I'm Sonia. My friends and I are planting a garden.
Gardens are magical places. Thousands of plants
bloom together, but every flower, every berry, and
every leaf is different. Each has a different smell,
different color, different shape, and different purpose.
Some flowers need lots of sunlight; others thrive in the
shade. Some have to be trimmed regularly, while others
are better off left alone. Some trees and flowers are
more fragile, and others are more hardy.

Kids are all different too. Some of us are in a hurry, and others take more time. Some of us seem shy and quiet, while others are chatty and loud. Some of our differences are easy to spot. Others take longer to notice. Each of us grows in our own way, so if you are curious about other kids, **JUST ASK!**

Not everyone is comfortable answering questions about themselves, but I don't mind. What am I doing? Several times a day, I prick my finger to measure the sugar in my blood, and I give myself shots of medicine called insulin. I do this because I have diabetes and my body doesn't make insulin naturally like other people's.

Even though this can sometimes hurt, I gather all of my courage to do it to be healthy.

Do you ever need to take medicine to be healthy?

I do. My name is **Rafael** and I have asthma, which means I sometimes have trouble breathing. When that happens, I take a break and use an inhaler with medicine to make breathing easier. Quiet time helps me slow down and catch my breath.

My inhaler is like a tool to help my body. Do you use a tool to help your body?

I'm **Anthony**, and I use a wheelchair to get around. Even though I can't run with my legs, I can go super fast!

How do you get
from place to place?

My name is **Madison**, and my guide dog Lucky helps me get places safely because I'm blind. My friend **Arturo** is blind too; he uses a cane to get around. Even though we can't see, we strengthen our other senses and notice lots of details others may miss; we can hear with our ears, smell with our noses, and feel with our hands.

How do you use
your senses?

I'm **Vijay.** I learn about the world differently because I can see, but I can't hear—I'm Deaf. Most of the time I communicate with people using my face and hands through sign language. It's cool to know another language.

I also love reading and writing. What about you?

I'm **Bianca** and I have dyslexia, so I have to work really hard and take my time when I am reading and writing words. Sometimes I use computer programs to help me. I love learning by doing things. My imagination is full of ideas, and I'm very good at making art from the pictures I see in my mind.

Are you really good
at something?

I'm great at dinosaurs—I know all about them!
I'm Jordan, and I have autism. Organizing and
counting all my toy dinosaurs again and again makes
me feel calm. My classmate Tiana also has
autism, but it's different for her. She doesn't talk.

But I like to talk. I especially like to talk
about dinosaurs.

What do you like
to talk about?

For me listening comes more easily than talking—and I'm a really good listener. My name is **Anh** and I speak with a stutter, so I sometimes repeat a word or get stuck when I try to say it. It may take me a little longer to express myself, and sometimes I'm too shy to talk, but I understand everything that's going on.

Do you ever wonder if people understand you?

I do. My name is Julia. Sometimes I wiggle or make sounds that I can't control, because I have Tourette's syndrome. People may look at me funny because they think I am not paying attention or just acting out. But it's not true; I am listening.

I don't always like having to explain—it frustrates me—but it helps when I tell people that it's just what my body does.

Do you ever
feel frustrated?

My name is **Manuel** and I have attention-deficit/hyperactivity disorder—it is also called ADHD. I can get frustrated when I really feel the need to move around even though I'm supposed to sit still. When my teachers and friends are patient with me if I forget something or get distracted, I can get myself back on track.

What's helpful to you?

I'm **Nolan.** It's helpful to me when the food I eat has a clear label that says it is nut-free, because I am allergic to nuts—they can make me so sick that I would have to go to the hospital if I ate any, even by accident. So I always tell people about my allergy and ask if any food has nut ingredients. Speaking up keeps me healthy.

How do you use your voice?

I love to sing, and I love to talk. I love to make new friends and be included. I am **Grace**. I was born with Down syndrome. Kids like me with Down syndrome have an extra building block called a chromosome in our bodies. But we are all different from each other too. I can do almost anything any other kid can do, though learning new things can take some time.

One way I learn is to ask questions.

What helps you learn?

It's me, Sonia, again!

I ask questions too! When something seems different or new I just ask my parents or my teachers and they help me to understand, especially if my friends don't feel ready to explain. This is what I've learned:

Imagine if all of the plants in this garden were exactly the same—like what if we only could grow peas? That would mean no strawberries or cucumbers or carrots. It might also mean no trees or roses or sunflowers.

Just like in our garden, all the ways we are different make our neighborhood—our whole world really—more interesting and fun. And just like all of these plants, each of us has unique powers to share with the world and make it more interesting and richer.

What will you do
with your powers?

ACKNOWLEDGMENTS

Kamala "Mala" Gururaja inspired me to write this book about children who live with challenging conditions but whose courage, determination, and grit sustains them every day.

Some children in my life may see their names in this book. Yes, it is you who provided a model for my story, but the children in this book are their own little people.

This book is aided immeasurably by my collaboration with and assistance from Ruby Shamir. Ruby, I thank you for not letting me give up on my vision for this book. As always, the insights of my friend Zara Houshmand improve the quality of all I write.

Rafael López is an extraordinary illustrator with whom I am honored to have worked. His drawings are done with love and caring for each child portrayed.

My gratitude is deep to my talented, patient, and sensitive editor at Penguin Random House, Jill Santopolo, and the entire team who worked on editing, producing, and promoting this book.

The sage advice of Peter and Amy Bernstein of the Bernstein Literary Agency, and of my lawyers, John S. Siffert and Mark A. Merriman, is always invaluable. My assistants Susan Anastasi, Anh Le, and Victoria Gómez are integral to all I do, and I am grateful to them.

It is impossible to describe the efforts of the many people who read and commented on my various drafts of this book and the organization that shared information. Many of the people are friends, but many others are professionals who graciously extended their expertise to help the accuracy of my portrayals. I thank all of you for the treasure of suggestions, ideas, and knowledge. I list in alphabetical order: Brooke Adler, Jenny Anderson, Diane Artaiz, Autism Speaks, Theresa Bartenope, Talia Benamy, Jed Bennett, David Briggs, Rachael Caggiano, Jennifer Callahan, Dr. Rebecca Carlin, Tricia Cecil, Sharon Darrow, Dr. Andrew Drexler, Cheryl Eissing, Suzanne Foger, Lisa Foster, Miriam Gonzerelli (my teacher cousin), Aurelia Grayson, Matthew Grieco, Dr. Kristen Harmon, Alejandro Herrera, Trish Ignacio, Robert A. Katzmann, Denise Konnari, Elizabeth Lunn, Dr. Alison May, Marisa Herrera Postlewate, Amy Richard, Dr. Corinne Rivera (my cousin Miriam's daughter), Dr. Carol Robertson, Dr. Dimitra Robokos, Ricki Seidman, Dr. Juan Sotomayor (my brother), Kristine Thompson, and C.J. Volpe.

PHILOMEL BOOKS
An imprint of Penguin Random House LLC
New York

LIBRARY OF CONGRESS CATALOGING-IN-PUBLICATION DATA IS AVAILABLE UPON REQUEST.

ISBN 9780525514121
Manufactured in China by RR Donnelley Asia Printing Solutions Ltd.
18

Edited by Jill Santopolo.   Design by Jennifer Chung.
Text set in OpenDyslexic.
The art was done in pencil, watercolor, and acrylic on paper and then manipulated digitally.